To Jane Langton, who has great skills with No-No Birds.
AFP and PP

For Lis, thank you for all your love and constant support.
My love, Jim

The No-No Bird copyright © Frances Lincoln Limited 2008
Text copyright © Andrew Fusek Peters and Polly Peters 2008
Illustrations copyright © Jim Coplestone 2008

First published in Great Britain in 2008 and in the USA in 2009 by
Frances Lincoln Children's Books,
4 Torriano Mews, Torriano Avenue, London NW5 2RZ

www.franceslincoln.com

British Library Cataloguing in Publication Data available on request

ISBN: 978-1-84507-810-2

Printed in Singapore

1 3 5 7 9 8 6 4 2

The No-No Bird

Andrew Fusek Peters and Polly Peters

Illustrated by Jim Coplestone

F

FRANCES LINCOLN
CHILDREN'S BOOKS

There was a bird, not long ago,
Whose favourite word was No! No! No!

"**No!**" he said to brushing hair,
"**No!**" to coats he wouldn't wear.

So many times he said this word,
That soon his name was No-No Bird.

Well, **No-No Bird** went out one day,
Proudly walking on his way.

Soon, he met a little mouse
Who ran out from her
little house.

"Who are you?" she said. "Do stay,
Would you like to come and play?"

But **No No Bird** just shook his head.
"No! **No! No!**" he loudly said.

"Silly Mouse! Have you not heard?
I'm the famous **No-No Bird!**"

At that, the Mouse began to cry!
"You're very rude," she sniffed,
"GOODBYE."

The path led deeper through the wood
And up ahead, a squirrel stood.

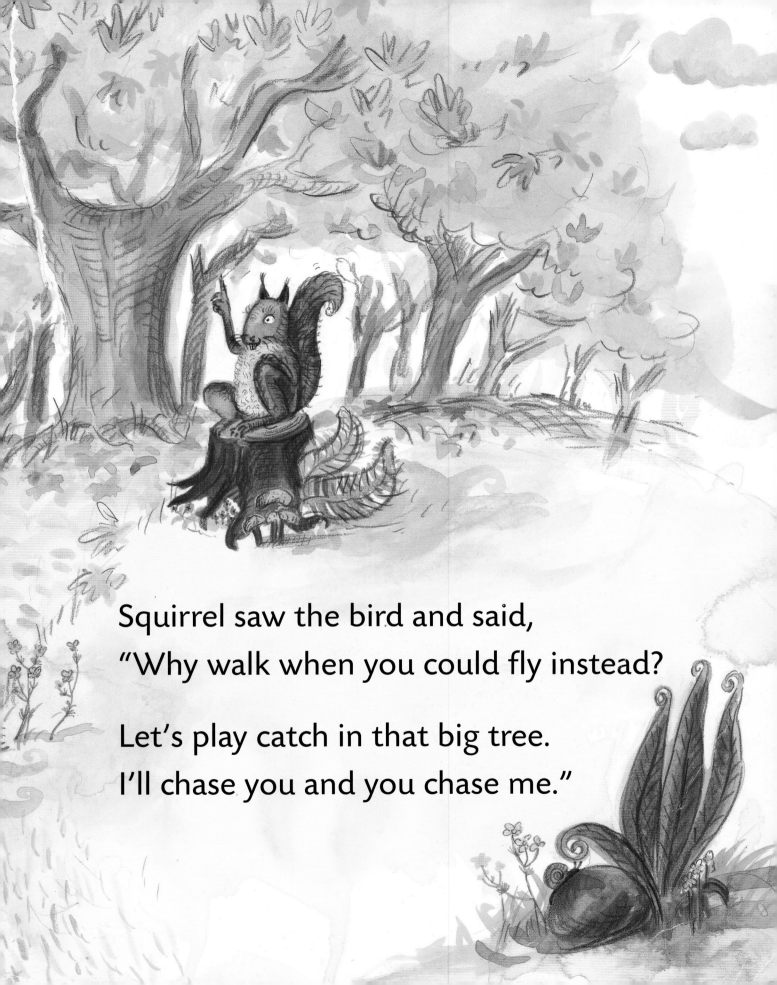

Squirrel saw the bird and said,
"Why walk when you could fly instead?

Let's play catch in that big tree.
I'll chase you and you chase me."

Bird stood still and tapped his toe,
Shook his head and just said, "**No!**"

"Funny Bird," laughed Squirrel, "why?
Is there a problem? Can't you fly?"

But Bird just said, "Have you not heard? I'm the famous **No-No Bird**."

And off he walked until a sound
Of **hissing** rose up from the ground.

It was a snake whose smile was wide
Enough to fit a bird inside...

He flicked his tail around Bird's leg.

"Ju-s-s-s-t s-s-stay a moment pleas-s-se, I beg."

No-No Bird stood still and sighed,
"You don't know who I am!"
he cried.

"That's right!" said Snake quite hungrily,
"So tell me now, because, you see,
My favourite food, I'm sure you've heard,
Is quite delicious...

No-No Bird!"

"Ah!" said Bird, "Um. Well. **Oh dear**."

But suddenly his mind was clear.
"The No-No Bird," he said, "is rare.
I haven't seen one anywhere!"

"Hmm," said Snake, "that's such a shame,
But you still haven't said YOUR name."

"Well," said Bird, "I WILL tell you...

...another time!" And up he flew,

Swiftly flapping fast as fear
Straight back home to Mother-dear.

"Goodness! You were quick!" she said.
Bird nodded once, then hung his head.

"I think you'd better come right here
And have a little cuddle, dear!"

And as he climbed upon her knee,
Bird said quietly, "I agree."

Could anyone believe their ears?

Were there tantrums?

Were there tears?

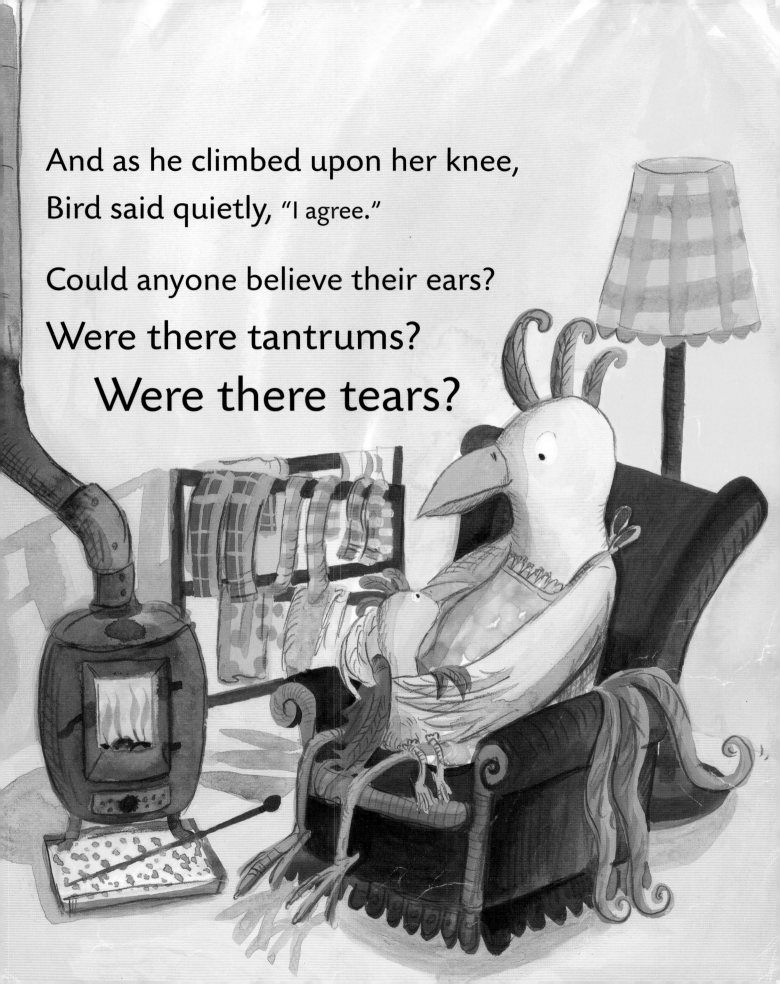

Mother smiled and hugged her bird.
"Do you **still** have a favourite word?"
She asked him as they cuddled tight.
And Bird looked up and said, "I might.

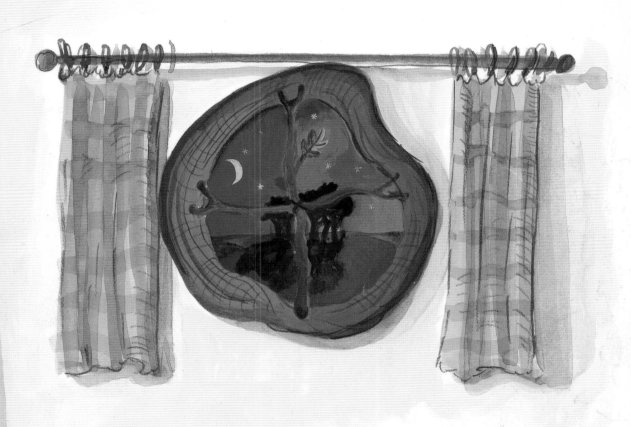

I found out something new today.
I didn't get to stop and play.
I didn't make a single friend,
And nearly met a sticky end."

Bird smiled and said, "So can you guess?
I've changed my favourite word to…

YES!"